ALI THE GREAT
Saves the Day

by SAADIA FARUQI   illustrated by DEBBY RAHMALIA

PICTURE WINDOW BOOKS
a capstone imprint

For Mubashir —SF
For Alesha —DR

Published by Picture Window Books, an imprint of Capstone
1710 Roe Crest Drive
North Mankato, Minnesota 56003
capstonepub.com

Text copyright © 2025 by Saadia Faruqi.
Illustrations copyright © 2025 by Capstone.

All rights reserved. No part of this publication may be reproduced in whole or in part, or stored in a retrieval system, or transmitted in any form or by any means, electronic, mechanical, photocopying, recording, or otherwise, without written permission of the publisher.

Library of Congress Cataloging-in-Publication Data is available on the Library of Congress website.

ISBN: 9780756593964 (paperback)
ISBN: 9780756593971 (ebook PDF)

Summary: Ali Tahir is a Pakistani American second grader who loves his family and friends—and also loves getting attention! Ali's big ideas sometimes lead to a little trouble—but his clever solutions and kind heart always save the day. Whether he's at the South Asian market, the dinosaur museum, a rainy indoor recess, or an Eid party in his own backyard, Ali is always discovering new things.

Designers: Kay Fraser and Tracy Davies

TABLE OF CONTENTS

ALI THE GREAT
AND THE MARKET MISHAP............................ 6

ALI THE GREAT
AND THE PAPER AIRPLANE FLOP............. 28

ALI THE GREAT
AND THE DINOSAUR MISTAKE................... 50

ALI THE GREAT
AND THE EID PARTY SURPRISE.................. 72

LET'S LEARN SOME URDU!

Ali and his family speak both English and Urdu, a language from Pakistan. Now you'll know some Urdu too!

ABBA (ah-BAH)—father (also baba)

AMMA (ah-MAH)—mother (also mama)

BHAI (BHA-ee)—brother

DADA (DAH-dah)—grandfather on father's side

DADI (DAH-dee)—grandmother on father's side

SALAAM (sah-LAHM)—hello

SHUKRIYA (shuh-KREE-yuh)—thank you

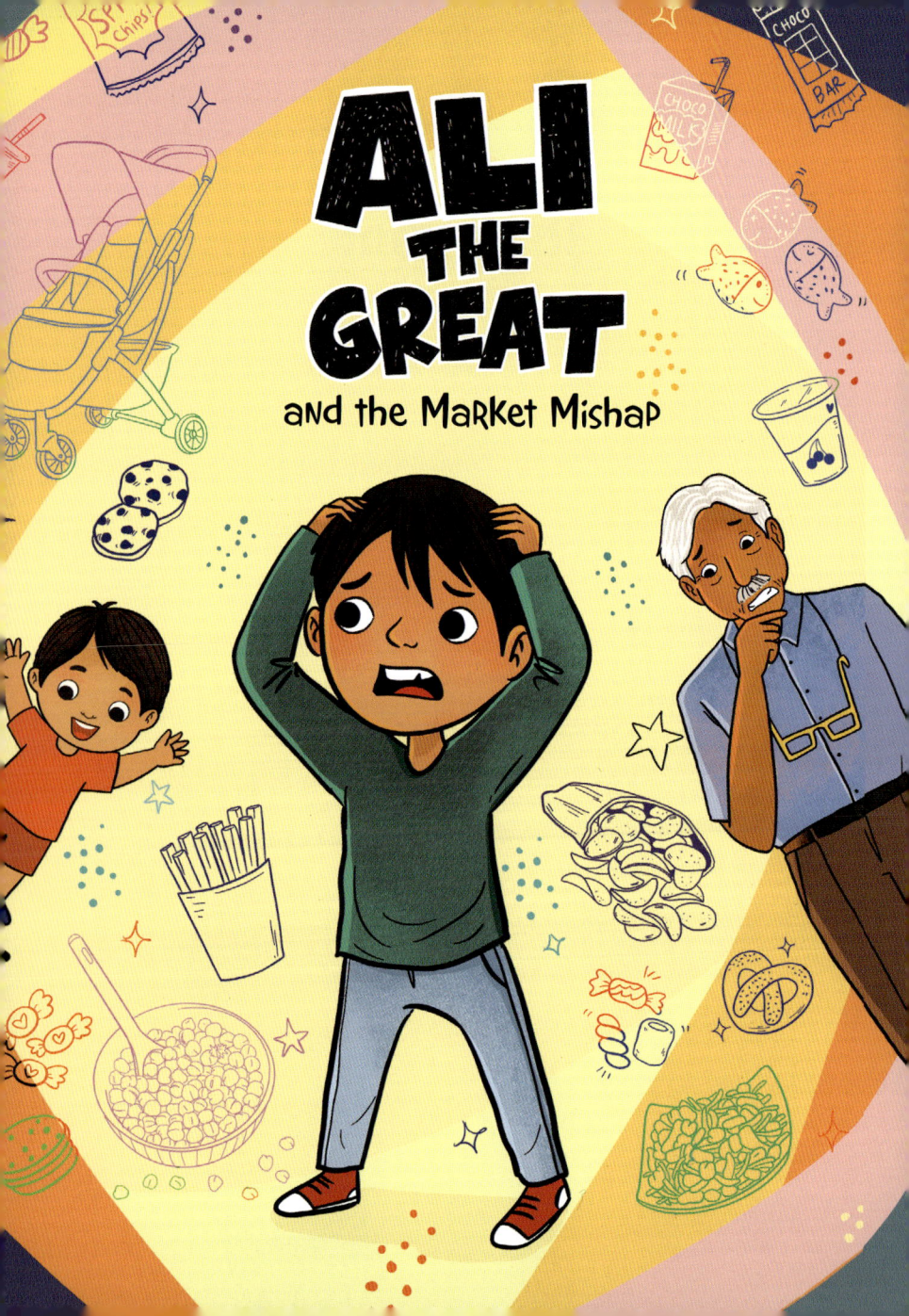

Chapter 1

WE NEED SNACKS

The rain had finally stopped.

"I'm all out of snacks," Dada announced.

Dada was Ali's favorite person. Dada and Dadi, Ali's grandparents, lived with his family.

Ali grinned. "A growing boy needs snacks too!" He loved crackers with cheese. And tiny pizza rolls. And cookies!

But Dada loved Pakistani snacks, because that's where he was from.

Dada snapped his fingers. "How about a trip to the market?" he said.

"Hooray!" Going out with Dada was always fun.

Ali grabbed his shoes. Dada helped Ali's little brother, Fateh, into his stroller.

"You better not get in any trouble, mister!" Dada teased Fateh.

Fateh just laughed. One thing Fateh was good at was trouble.

"I'll keep an eye on him, Dada!" Ali said proudly. "That's what big brothers do."

They walked on the sidewalk. At least, *Dada* walked. Fateh wiggled in his stroller. Ali jumped over puddles as he counted them.

"Ten!" Ali shouted.

"Careful, Ali!" Dada warned.

Ali grinned. "I'm always careful!"

Chapter 2

THE MARKET

The South Asian market was very big.

They headed inside and left Fateh's stroller at the front. Ali loved the market. He looked around in awe.

"Amazing . . . ," Ali whispered.

They passed the vegetable carts and the frozen foods section. Ali saw lots of cold soda bottles and huge bags of rice. There was even a section of colorful toys.

"Keep an eye on your brother—and look for those chips I like, please," Dada said as they reached the snack area. Then he continued down the aisle to find the things on his list.

"Uh-huh," said Ali.

There were hundreds of snacks on the shelves. Crispy nimko. Sweet and spicy candy. Salty chickpeas.

Then Ali saw a big display of spicy chips.

"Gimme!" Fateh shouted.

Oops, thought Ali. Fateh loved chips, just like Dada.

"You can't have these, buddy," he said. "Too spicy."

Fateh didn't listen. He let go of Ali's hand and ran straight at the display.

Ali leaped forward and grabbed the cardboard display before it tipped over.

Phew! Those were some cool moves!

"Thank you very much!" Ali said and took a bow, even though nobody was around.

Wait, where was Fateh?

☆ Chapter 3 ☆

THE RESCUE

Ali knew he had to find his little brother, fast! He ran down the snack aisle, past a store clerk. No Fateh.

He went to the front of the store and looked inside the stroller.

Sometimes Fateh liked to hide in there. Nope.

"Fateh!" Ali whispered loudly. "Where are you?"

There was no reply. Ali gulped. This was bad. Very, very bad. Dada would be so mad that Ali had lost his little brother.

Then Ali saw a ladder.

Yes! He got a brilliant idea. He climbed up the ladder and craned his neck. From up high, Ali could see the whole store! He looked so hard his eyes hurt.

"Hey—be careful!" a store clerk called out.

Just then, Ali saw Fateh's red shirt in the toy section. He jumped down and ran through the aisles.

There was Fateh, sitting between two shelves. "Come here, silly goose!" Ali said and reached for him.

"No!" Fateh yelled.

Ali looked around and saw the spicy chips. He grabbed one and dangled it in front of Fateh. "Come get it!"

Fateh's eyes grew big. "Gimme!" he said and toddled toward Ali.

"Gotcha!" Ali picked up his brother and held him close. "No more exploring for you."

They met Dada at the checkout counter.

"Ah, Fateh found the spicy chips for us!" Dada said and put the bag in his cart.

Ali nodded. "Oh yes, he was a *big* help," he said.

Fateh smiled.

BORED

It was raining outside. Ali's class was stuck in the gym for recess.

"I'm so bored!" Ali groaned.

"Yeah," Zack agreed. "There's nothing to do inside!"

Yasmin saw some boxes and peeked inside. "Ooh, art supplies!" she said. She took out some paper and crayons and started coloring.

Ali thought coloring was boring. He watched Yasmin work. Was there something fun he could do with that paper?

"I know!" Ali suddenly shouted.

"Let's make paper airplanes!"

Yasmin looked up and frowned. "I don't know how."

Ali grinned. "Don't worry," he said. "I'll help you. I'm an expert!"

He took a piece of paper and folded it carefully. Once, twice, three times. He made sure the creases were very sharp.

Ta-da! Ali held up his paper airplane.

"Cool!" Zack said. "Can you please make me one too?"

"Me too!" said Emma.

☆ Chapter 2 ☆

THE CONTEST

Ali took more papers from the box and folded more airplanes.

He didn't rush. He had to be careful and neat. If he made a mistake, the airplane wouldn't fly as far.

Soon, there was a pile of airplanes for his friends to choose from.

Yasmin grabbed her crayons. "I'm going to make a design on mine!" she said.

"Great idea!" Ali replied. Art wasn't boring when there were planes involved!

Ali added white racing stripes to his. Yasmin drew flowers on hers. Emma's had polka dots. Zack's had a fire-breathing dragon!

Then Ali showed his friends how to fly their planes.

"You have to hold up your plane like this and lean forward," he said. "And you have to throw hard."

"Let's have a contest!" Zack suggested. "Whoever's plane flies the farthest wins!"

"Okay!" Ali said. He was the pro, and he was ready!

Emma went first. Her plane flew toward the basketball hoop. "Yay!" she said.

Then it was Zack's turn. His plane went even farther. "Beat that!" Zack said.

Yasmin was third. She smiled nervously.

"You can do it, Yasmin!" Ali cheered.

Yasmin aimed carefully then threw. Her plane landed all the way in the bleachers!

"Wow!" everyone cried.

AND THE WINNER IS...

Finally, it was Ali's turn. He wasn't worried. He built the best airplanes. He would definitely win!

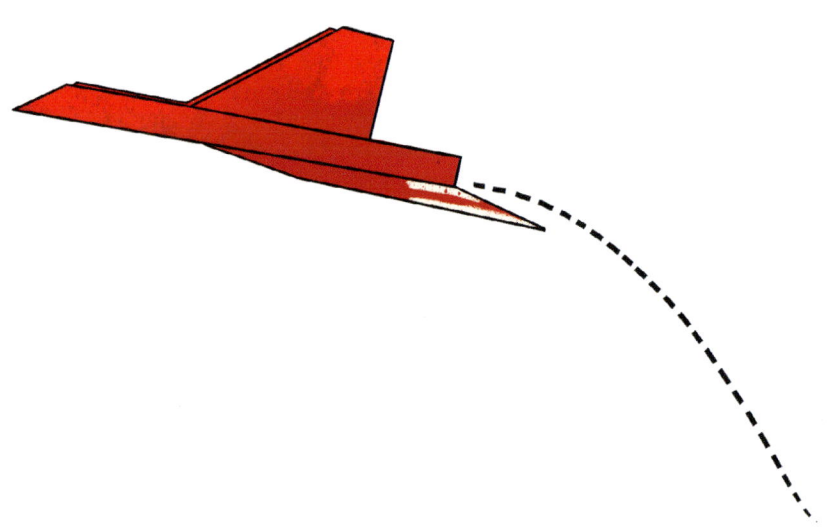

Ali threw his paper airplane with all his might. It soared high up. Then it dipped down. Then it looped and twisted!

Everyone watched the airplane. It looped once more. Then it landed . . . right behind Ali.

"Oh no!" Ali cried. This was terrible. He wasn't the winner. He came in last!

"I lost?" he said, surprised.

"No, you didn't, Ali," Yasmin said. "You're the winner, with me!"

"I am?" Ali asked.

Emma nodded. "She's right! You made our airplanes for us," she said.

"And you taught us the best way to fly," Zack added.

Ali started to feel better. He *did* know the most about building paper airplanes.

Yasmin clapped. "We both win!" she cheered loudly.

"Teamwork!" Zack said, even louder.

Ali pointed to the box of supplies.

"Ready for another round?" he asked.

"Bring it on, co-pilot!" Yasmin replied.

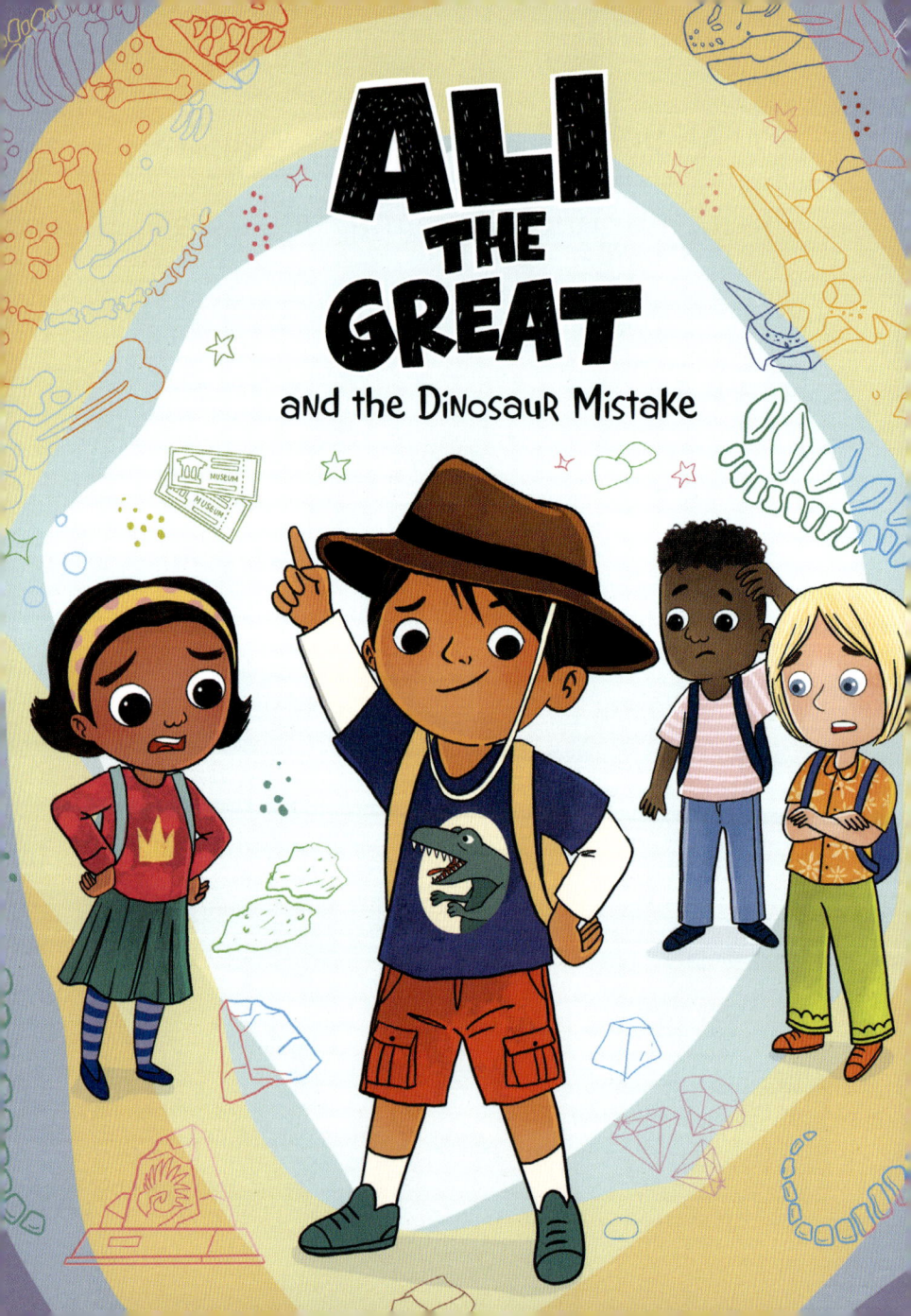

☆ Chapter 1 ☆

THE MUSEUM

Today was a very special day. Ms. Alex's second grade class was at the museum. It was a big, shiny building with gardens all around.

"This is so cool!" Ali said as he climbed off the bus.

"I love museums," Yasmin said. "We can learn all sorts of things here!"

Ali grinned. "Too late for me. I already know everything."

Yasmin laughed.

Ms. Alex made them all stand in a line. "You must be on your best behavior, students!" she told them.

"We will!" Emma replied, smiling.

A volunteer met them in the lobby. "I'm Taylor," he said. "Please be sure to follow museum rules at all times."

"Rules?" Ali whispered. He thought rules were boring. He liked doing things his way.

"No running or jumping. No eating or drinking. No touching the exhibits," Taylor said. "Especially the dinosaurs."

Ali's eyes grew wide. "I love dinosaurs!" he cried. "I know all about them!"

☆ Chapter 2 ☆

PALEONTOLOGY

Taylor showed the students around. They saw mummies from ancient Egypt. "So creepy!" Zack said.

Then they saw minerals and gems. "So beautiful," Emma said.

They spent a long time reading facts about the human body.

"Did you know we have 206 bones in our body?" Yasmin asked.

"Yes, I know that!" Ali said impatiently. "But where are the dinosaurs?"

Finally, Taylor led them to the paleontology exhibit.

Ali looked around with his mouth open. Huge dinosaur skeletons reached up to the ceiling. "Whoa!" he whispered.

"Pa-le-on-to-lo-gy," Yasmin read from the sign.

"That means the study of dinosaurs," Ali told her. He'd read it in a book about dinosaurs that Abba had given him.

"Correct," Taylor replied. "Dinosaurs lived millions of years ago, before humans and most other animals."

Ali already knew that too. "Look, a T. rex!" he shouted, pointing to a huge dinosaur.

"Whoa!" Zack said.

Taylor held up his hand.

"Actually, that's an allosaurus."

"I thought you knew everything," Zack teased Ali.

Ali shrugged. "It was just a mistake."

Taylor pointed to another big skeleton. "*That's* the T. rex," he said. "Do you know what it liked to eat?"

"Plants!" Ali said quickly. But wait, T. rex was the biggest, baddest dinosaur. Maybe Ali was wrong about the plants?

"T. rex ate other dinosaurs!" Zack shouted.

"Correct!" Taylor replied. "T. rex was a meat eater."

Ali scowled. He was supposed to be the dinosaur expert, not Zack!

☆ Chapter 3 ☆

MISTAKES ARE OKAY

"Do you think there are any dinosaurs left in the world today?" Taylor asked the students.

Ali rolled his eyes. What a silly question. He definitely knew the answer to this one. "Of course not. They're all extinct now."

Taylor shook his head. "Actually, birds are a type of dinosaur."

Ali looked at the floor. "Oh, yeah," he whispered. He was embarrassed about his mistakes. He wasn't an expert at all!

Taylor came over to him. "Don't worry, buddy. It's okay to get things wrong."

Ali looked up. "Really?"

"Yup," Taylor replied. "Scientists often make mistakes. But they learn from them and do better next time."

Ali grinned. "Then I'm a scientist for sure. My mistakes are expert-level!"

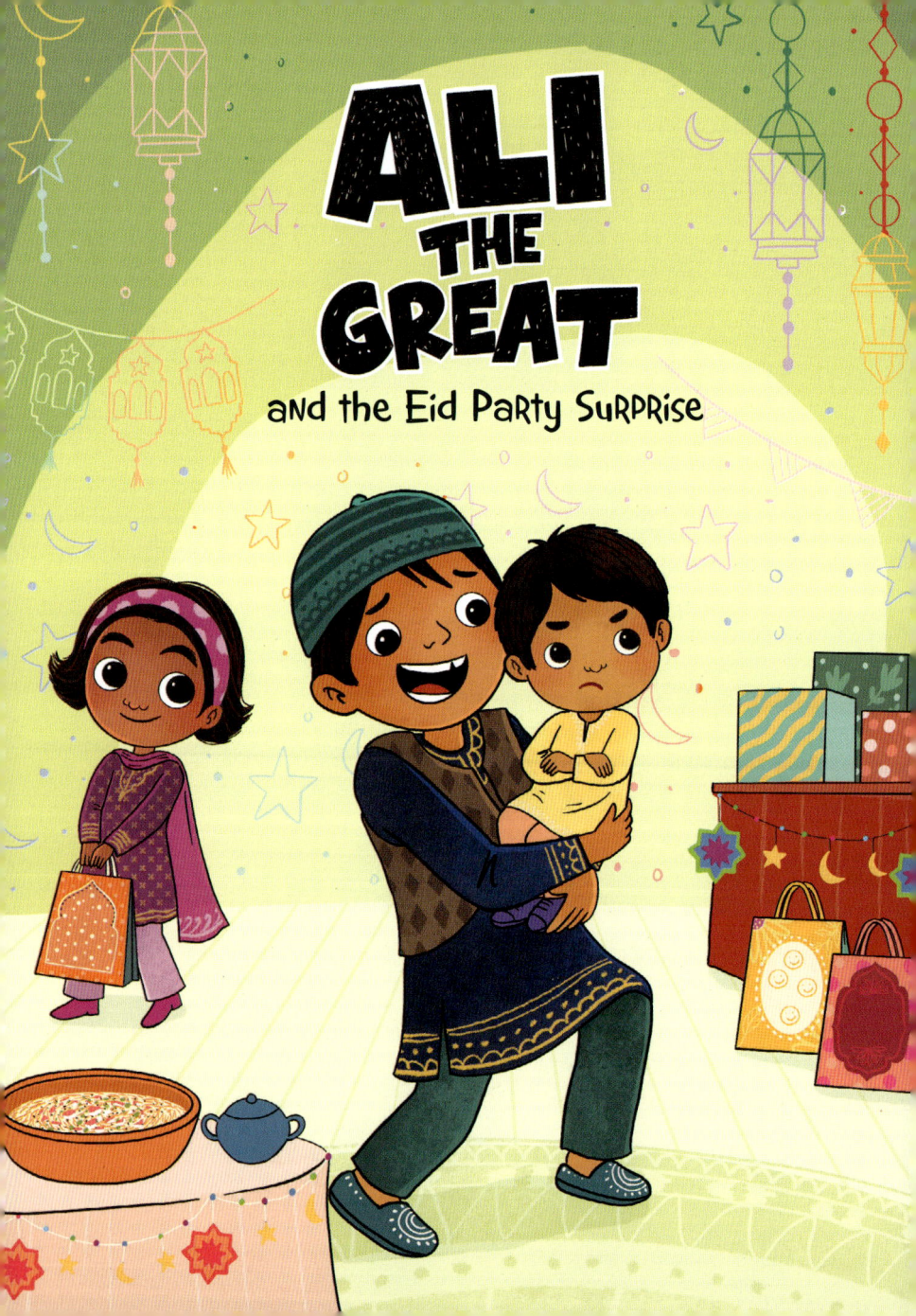

Chapter 1

EID DAY

Ali woke up bright and early. "It's Eid day!" he shouted.

He got dressed and tidied his room. Amma liked the whole house to be clean for Eid. Ali gathered up his juggling balls, books, cars, and other toys and shoved them under the bed. Done!

Amma and Abba were already in the kitchen. "Looks like someone is excited," Amma said, smiling.

Of course Ali was excited. Eid was the best day of the year! It came at the end of Ramadan. Eid meant visits with family and friends, and getting lots of presents.

Best of all, Ali's family always had an Eid party in the afternoon. It was going to be so much fun!

After breakfast, Ali raced back to his room to get dressed. He wore his new shalwar kameez and fancy shoes.

Dada met him downstairs.

"Looking spiffy," Dada said.

"We match!" Ali pointed out.

All the boys matched. Even Fateh.

Amma showed Ali the henna on her hands. It was beautiful. "Wow!" Ali said.

"Me!" Fateh shouted. He wanted henna on his hands too.

"Not for you," Ali told him.

"You're in charge of your little brother today," Amma reminded Ali.

"Yes, ma'am!" Ali replied.

Fateh pouted.

☆ Chapter 2 ☆

MISBEHAVING BROTHER

Fateh was in a cranky mood. He cried as they drove to the mosque to pray.

Ali's family prayed with their friends. Then they hugged each  other and said, "Eid Mubarak!"

Fateh ran around in the grass. He threw his goody bag on the ground and stomped on it. Then he cried because he'd broken his toys and candy.

"Behave, Fateh!" Ali whispered. "You're spoiling all the Eid fun."

"No!" Fateh shouted. Then he ran off with Ali's candy.

Ali sighed and went after his brother.

When they got home, it was time to get ready for the Eid party. Abba set up tables and chairs in the backyard.

Ali helped.

Fateh didn't.

Amma brought out plates of food. "Our guests will be here soon," she said.

Fateh crawled under a chair and pretended to be a lion in a pen. "Roar!"

"Good kitty," Ali said.

Ali's friend Yasmin was the first to arrive. "Eid Mubarak!" she said. She handed Ali a giant box wrapped in colorful paper.

"Thanks!" Ali said and handed a present to Yasmin. "Amma says we can open gifts after dinner."

"Want to play tag?" Yasmin asked.

Just then, Fateh let out a cry as his chair tipped over.

Ali rolled his eyes. "Maybe later, Yasmin," he said.

☆ Chapter 3 ☆

JUGGLING FUN

Ali's parents were busy with the guests. Dada was on barbecue duty. Dadi was refilling water glasses. Ali was in charge of Fateh.

What would make his brother happy?

He thought of Fateh pretending to be a lion. That made him think of the circus. He snapped his fingers. "I'll be right back!"

He ran to his room and came back with a bag.

"Ladies and gentlemen!" Ali cried. "Welcome to Fateh's Eid Circus! It's time for Ali the juggler!"

All the kids sat and watched as Ali pulled three balls out of the bag. He tossed them high up in the air—one, two, three! Then he added one more.

The balls circled round and round as Ali juggled, higher and higher. He watched them carefully. Juggling was fun, but it took a lot of concentration.

"Ooh!" Fateh yelled. "Gimme!"

Ali tossed the balls high above his head one last time. Then, one by one, he caught them all and handed them to Fateh.

"You're so good at that!" Yasmin said.

Everyone clapped loudly. Ali grinned and bowed. "Thank you, thank you!" he said.

After dinner, Amma handed out a special Eid dessert called sawaiyan. It was Ali's favorite.

"Good job today," Amma whispered to him. Ali smiled.

Then it was time for the gift exchange. Ali got a magic show set, a jigsaw puzzle, and lots of books.

"Next Eid, you can add some magic tricks to your act," Dada said.

Ali looked at Fateh. "You can be my assistant," he said.

"Gimme!" Fateh said, and everyone laughed.

EID MUBARAK!

- Eid is an Arabic word meaning "festival" or "feast."

- Muslims celebrate two Eids each year: Eid al-Fitr and Eid al-Adha.

- Eid al-Fitr celebrates the end of Ramadan. Eid al-Adha marks the sacrifice of Abraham. Both are joyous occasions.

- On Eid day, Muslims celebrate with prayer, food, family gatherings, and lots of fun!

- During Eid, you can wish a Muslim "Happy Eid!" or "Eid Mubarak!"

WHAT DO YOU THINK?

- Ali likes to learn dinosaur facts. Is there a topic that you consider yourself an "expert" on? Write five facts about a topic that you know well.

- Co-pilots are people who share the work and responsibility of flying a plane. The word "co-pilot" can also mean partner in a project or adventure. Think of a project or activity you would like to try. Who would you choose as your co-pilot, and why?

- Ali's family celebrates Eid. Do you also celebrate Eid or have friends who do? What special days does your family celebrate?

JOKING AROUND!

What do you call a dinosaur that's sleeping?
a dino-snore

How does a hen measure her eggs?
egg-zactly

What sort of fish belongs in a circus?
a clown fish

Why did the airplane get sent to its room?
It had a bad altitude.

About the Author

Saadia Faruqi is a Pakistani American writer, interfaith activist, and cultural sensitivity trainer featured in *O, The Oprah Magazine*. Author of the Yasmin chapter book series, Saadia also writes middle grade novels, such as *Yusuf Azeem Is Not a Hero*, and other books for children. Saadia is editor-in-chief of *Blue Minaret*, an online magazine of poetry, short stories, and art. Besides writing, she also loves reading, binge-watching her favorite shows, and taking naps. She lives in Houston with her family.

About the Illustrator

Debby Rahmalia is an illustrator based in Indonesia with a passion for storytelling. She enjoys creating diverse works that showcase an array of cultures and people. Debby's long-term dream was to become an illustrator. She was encouraged to pursue her dream after she had her first baby and has been illustrating ever since. When she's not drawing, she spends her time reading the books she illustrated to her daughter or wandering around the neighborhood with her.